The Princess and the Wise Woman

Written by
Kana Riley

Illustrated by
Jenny Williams

Once upon a time, a princess sat by her window.

3

The princess looked out. She looked past a pine tree.

She looked down a long road.

She saw six high hills.

"Oh," said the princess. "I wish I could ride my bike over the six high hills. But the road is so long, and the hills are so high. I don't think I can make the trip."

7

So the princess just sat by
her window and wished.

A wise woman saw her. "Dear princess," she called. "Why are you sitting inside on this fine day?"

9

"Oh," said the princess. "I wish I could ride my bike over the six high hills. But the road is so long, and the hills are so high. I don't think I can make the trip."

10

The wise woman gave the princess a wise look. "I think I can help you," she said. "I will visit you for five days. For these five days, you must do what I say."

11

On Monday when the wise woman came, the princess did nine jumping jacks.

On Tuesday when the wise woman came, the princess skipped rope for five minutes.

13

On Wednesday when the wise woman came, the princess ran in place for fifteen minutes.

14

On Thursday when the wise woman came, the princess jogged to the pine tree.

15

On Friday when the wise woman came, the princess rode her bike to the pine tree and back.

The princess liked it so much, she did it again…

17

and again… and again.

18

"Now," said the wise woman, "you are ready for the trip."

"But the road is so long, and the hills are so high. I don't think I can make it," said the princess.

20

"Oh," said the wise woman, "I think you can."

So the princess rode her bike past the pine tree,

down the long road,

over the six high hills. And then she rode back again.